Published in the United States by Convergent Books, an imprint
of Random House, a division of Penguin Random House LLC, New York.

CONVERGENT BOOKS is a registered trademark, and its C colophon is
a trademark of Penguin Random House LLC.

ISBN 978-0-593-23469-3
Ebook ISBN 978-0-593-23470-9

The Library of Congress record is available at https://lccn.loc.gov/2021031174.

Printed in China

convergentbooks.com

10 9 8 7 6 5 4 3 2 1

First Edition

Book and cover design by Marysarah Quinn

A Family Prayer

WRITTEN BY
Shay Youngblood

ILLUSTRATED BY
Kristina Swarner

CONVERGENT

For

Stephanie, Johnathan, Cartillious,

Ursula, Schmohn, Charity,

and their children, and their children,

with love.

Author's Note

I grew up an only child in Georgia, my family extending to include those in my neighborhood, school, and church communities. Whether related by blood or not, an African American elder was called auntie or uncle. Young Black men and women called one another brother and sister. Kids my age called one another cousin because we felt as close as siblings.

Nearly three years old when my birth mother died, I was raised in the Southern Baptist Church by a community of mostly older women. We attended church every Sunday and sometimes during the week. I believed in the power of prayer and had faith in miracles. When I was very young, I consistently prayed for my mother to come back to me, and I prayed for siblings. When I was ten years old, I discovered I had an older brother and three younger sisters living in California with the father we shared. My prayers were answered, and we are connected to this day. Of course, my mother didn't come back to life, but I began to see the world differently. I looked around my community and appreciated the fact that I was blessed with nearly a dozen mothers!

During my childhood, prayer was an essential part of my nighttime ritual. Each evening after homework was done and my favorite television shows were over, I would wash my face, brush my teeth, and get into my pajamas. Before going to sleep, I would kneel beside my bed, fold my hands, close my eyes, and bow my head. My great-grandmother Nettie Mae and my great-aunt Luellen taught me short prayers that I recited each night, but then I would want to pray for everyone I knew: family members, neighbors, teachers, the lunch ladies in the cafeteria, and even cashiers at the grocery store. My prayers were long and sometimes elaborate. At first it was a way to keep the light on in the room a little longer. My prayers were sincere, but I was afraid of the dark, scared that monsters or snakes were under my bed and, most terrifying of all, that some harm might come to the people I loved. Prayer was a way for me to remember that God was watching over everyone I cared about.

When I got older, I no longer knelt beside my bed or said my prayers out loud. I realized that I could pray silently anywhere I wanted for as long as I wanted. Saying a silent prayer whenever I'm afraid comforts me to this day.

The people in my community gave me a strong sense of identity, values to live by, pride in my culture, and a sense of belonging. My hope is that children reading this book will feel the same sense of belonging in their own communities and see how prayer can lift them up as they pray for those they love.

Shay Youngblood

My mother is a blessing.

Keep her safe from harm.
When I wake up in the morning,
she shines brighter than the sun.
She listens to my hopes and dreams.
She watches over me while I sleep.

Mothers are a blessing.
Keep them safe and well.

My father is a blessing.

Keep him safe from harm.
He wraps me in the comfort of
stories about the big, wide world.
He teaches me to see that rainy days
   are lucky days.

Fathers are a blessing.
Keep them safe and well.

My grandmother is a blessing.

Keep her safe from harm.
She bakes buttery lemon pound cakes just for me.
Her kisses smell like ginger and cinnamon.
Her hands fold mine in prayer.
Our hearts are close even when we're far apart.

Grandmothers
are a blessing.
Keep them safe
and well.

My grandfather is a blessing.

Keep him safe from harm.
He knows the histories of the world,
telling fables and proverbs that guide me.
Nose-to-nose kisses are our special greeting.
His jokes make my belly shake.

Grandfathers are a blessing.
Keep them safe and well.

My sister
is a blessing.

Keep her safe from harm.
She keeps my secrets
and shows me how invisible ink
can reveal mysteries.
She helps me find my way.

*Sisters are a blessing.
Keep them safe
and well.*

My brother is a blessing.

Keep him safe from harm.
When we play chess like champions,
I earn every win.
He holds my hand when I'm afraid.
He never lets me fall.

Brothers are a blessing.
Keep them safe and well.

My auntie is a blessing.

Keep her safe from harm.
She sings sweet songs she
    learned long ago
from her mother, who sang
    to her at bedtime.
She whispers tales of her
    world travels
as she rocks me to sleep.

Aunties are a blessing.
Keep them safe and well.

My uncle is a blessing.

Keep him safe from harm.
We work side by side in his garden,
planting seeds that bring joy to the
family table.
Flowers bloom and vegetables grow.
He treats me to double scoops of ice
cream when it's just us two.

Uncles are a blessing.
Keep them safe and well.

My cousins are a blessing.

Keep them safe from harm.
They laugh the loudest at my knock-knock jokes.
When we're together, it's like parading in our own circus.
We have fun climbing trees, watching snails, and racing squirrels.

Cousins are a blessing.
Keep them safe and well.

My godparents
are a blessing.

Keep them safe from harm.
They were chosen for their kindness
    and their love for my family.
They give the best presents
and come to all my big events.

Godparents are a blessing.
Keep them safe and well.

**My babysitters
are a blessing.**

Keep them safe from harm.
They always care for me
and protect me.
They know the best games
to play
and make the tastiest
snacks.

Babysitters are
a blessing.
Keep them safe
and well.

My dog is a blessing.

Keep her safe from harm.
She protects us day and night.
Her funny tricks comfort us.
When we walk, she leads the way.

Pets are a blessing.
Keep them safe and well.

My family is a blessing.

Keep them safe from harm.
They show me love.
I love them too.
I'm thankful for them all.

Families are a blessing.
Keep them safe and well.

I am a blessing to my family.

I love them, each and every one.
When they are far away from me,
and I am far away from them,
my prayers surround us all with peace
    and love,
morning, noon, and night.

I am a blessing.
I am safe. I am well.
I am loved.

Acknowledgments

Many thanks to my agents, Tanya McKinnon and Carol Taylor, for their master classes and for giving me the opportunity to take on new challenges. And to my editors, Porscha Burke and Keren Baltzer, who both pivoted gracefully.

Much appreciation to my chosen family—my tribe and sustaining supporters of my choice to make a life of art. Everyone can't be named here, but there are souls and beloveds who remain close to my heart no matter how far the geographical distance: Angie Cruz, Christine Irving, Priscilla Hale, Veronica Chambers, Lazette Jackson, Julie Siegel, Delores Bushong, Marlene Johnson, Maggie Mermin, Eve Humphreys, Kay Hagan, Jackie Kelley; my sisters: Twonia Kelley-Dingle, Kathy Crosby, Mary Ruth Crosby, Lydia Crosby; my brother: William Crosby; Eric Lane, Laura Pirott-Quintero, Isabelle Bagshaw, Tina McElroy Ansa, Daniel Alexander Jones, Linda Bryant, Laurie Cubbin, Alane Freund, Valerie Boyd, Kelley Alexander, Miriam Phields, Veta Goler, and librarians around the world.

Georgia-born writer **Shay Youngblood** is the author of
the novels *Black Girl in Paris, Soul Kiss, Big Mama Stories*,
and *Mama's Home.* Her plays have been widely produced.
She is the recipient of numerous grants and awards including
the Pushcart Prize for fiction. She received her MFA in
creative writing from Brown University and has
taught creative writing at NYU and the City College
of New York. She currently lives in Atlanta.
www.shayyoungblood.com

At the age of five, **Kristina Swarner** decided that she
wanted to be an artist when she grew up. Since graduating
from the Rhode Island School of Design, Kristina has created
many award-winning illustrations and exhibited her
work internationally. She lives in Chicago with her
mostly four-legged family.

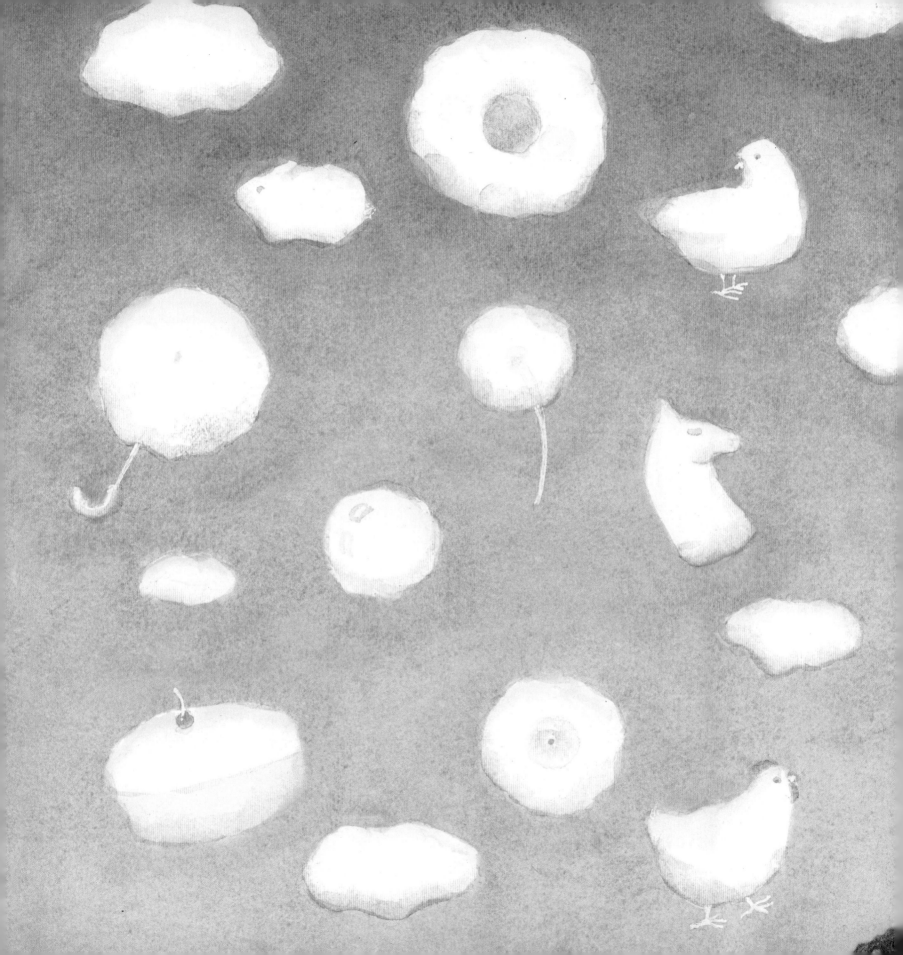